NORMAN
THE SLUG WHO SAVED CHRISTMAS

For Nia,
in appreciation of all the magic
you have brought to our books –
S and P x

SIMON AND SCHUSTER
First published in Great Britain in 2015
by Simon and Schuster UK Ltd
1st Floor, 222 Gray's Inn Road, London, WC1X 8HB
A CBS Company

A CIP catalogue record for this book is available
from the British Library upon request

978-1-4711-2098-5 (HB)
978-1-4711-7830-6 (PB)
978-1-4711-2099-2 (eBook)

Printed in China
1 3 5 7 9 10 8 6 4 2

NORMAN
THE SLUG WHO SAVED CHRISTMAS

SIMON AND SCHUSTER
London New York Sydney Toronto New Delhi

by Sue Hendra
and Paul Linnet

Norman was very excited. It was Christmas Eve.

His stocking was up and he'd even left
a snack for Father Christmas's reindeer.

Meanwhile, far above,
Father Christmas sneezed.

"ACHOO!"

And without him knowing it,
a sack fell from his sleigh!

Down on the ground, Norman snuggled in his bed.
"I hope I've been a good slug," he said to himself.
"I hope Father Christmas comes.

Yes, I have been a good slug," thought Norman.
And he was just closing his eyes when . . .

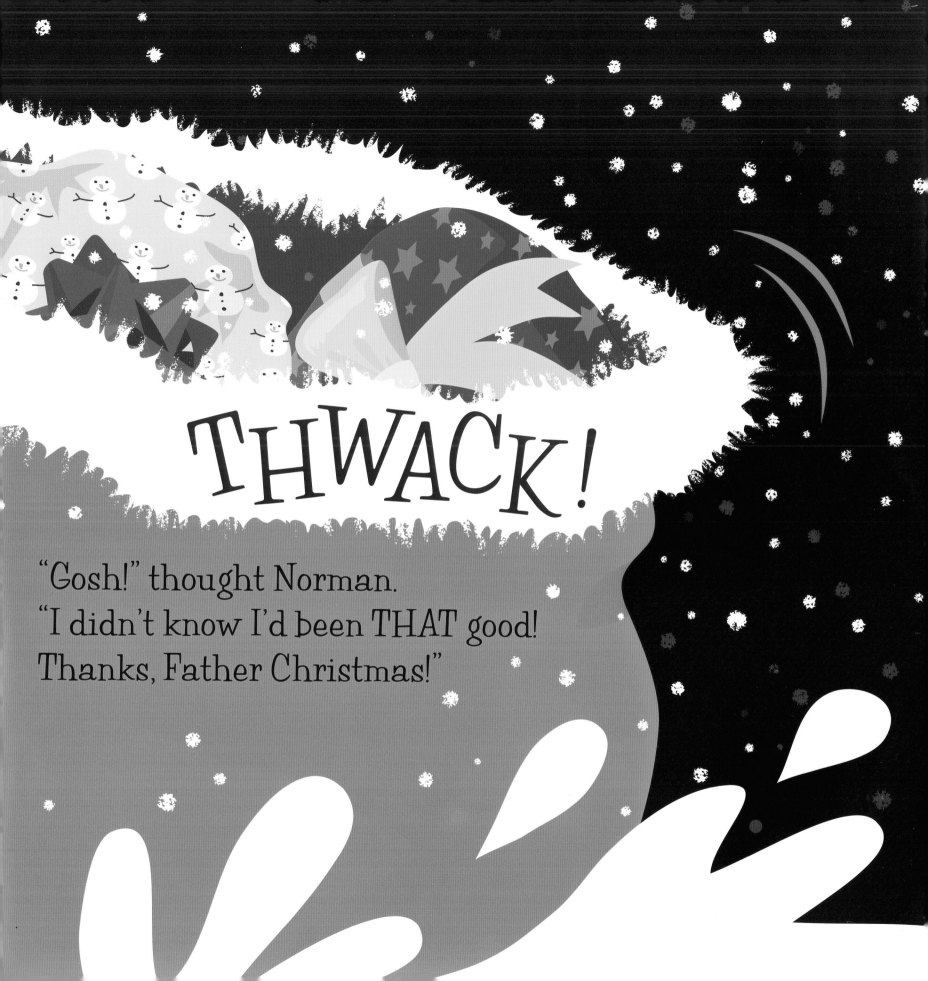

THWACK!

"Gosh!" thought Norman.
"I didn't know I'd been THAT good!
Thanks, Father Christmas!"

Norman dived straight in.
There was wrapping paper everywhere.

But then he spotted something.
"What's this label?" said Norman.

"The scooter is for Jess," he read.

"The ukulele is for Billy.

And the football is for Susie.

Oh no!
What have I done?

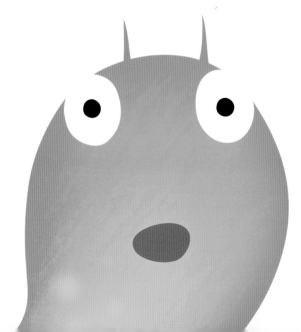

None of these presents are for me! Billy, Jess and Susie will wake up tomorrow and think that Father Christmas has forgotten them.

I'd better get these presents to Wiggleton as fast as I can."

The Shelby Family,
11 Slime Avenue,
Wiggleton

But Wiggleton looked a very long way away.
How would Norman get all the presents there?

And that's when he had an idea!

Heeeaavvve!
He pushed over the sign.

"Fantastic! That will do nicely," thought Norman.

Then he set to work gathering all the other things he needed.

He was very busy.

Ta-da!

Now it was time to re-wrap the presents.
But how? Norman didn't have any
sticky tape!

But luckily . . .

... if there's one thing slugs don't need, it's sticky tape.

With a slither and a slother,
the presents were ready!

Phew!

Now it was time to put his plan into action.

"Hey, snails!" he called. "I need your help. We need to deliver the Shelby family's presents or their Christmas will be ruined!"

"But Norman," said the puzzled snails. "How will we do that?"

"Like this!" said Norman.

"Giddy up!"

Finally they arrived at number 11 Slime Avenue.

"Er, Norman," said a snail. "How will you get to the chimney?"

"I won't," Norman replied.
"I'm going to use the cat flap!"
He heaved and pushed . . .

. . . until the last present was safely through. "Quick, Norman!" cried the snails. "THE CHILDREN ARE COMING!" Norman needed to hide. But where?

TA-DA!

Norman LOVED being a bauble.

And nobody would ever know that a slug had saved Christmas Day.